This book belongs to..

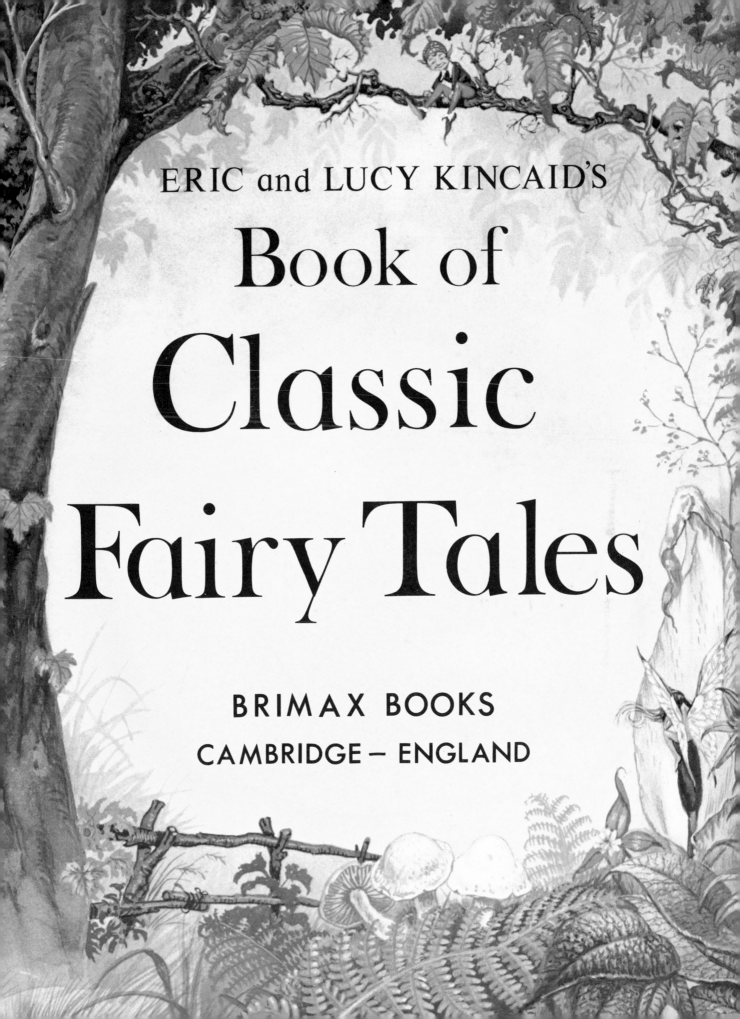

ERIC and LUCY KINCAID'S

Book of
Classic
Fairy Tales

BRIMAX BOOKS
CAMBRIDGE — ENGLAND

Rapunzel

One day, a Prince was riding in the forest
when he heard a girl singing. He got down
from his horse and led him quietly along a
mossy footpath until he came to a clearing.
In the clearing was a tower, as round and as
straight as a giant pine tree. At the very
top of the tower, which was so tall it looked
as though its roof was touching the sky, there
was a tiny window. It was from the tiny
window that the sound of the voice was coming.

"It will be a long climb up the stairs to
the top," said the Prince shading his eyes
and looking upwards, "but I must find out
who is singing so sweetly."

He looped the horse's bridle over a branch
and went to look for a way in. He walked
round the tower a hundred times. He could
find no door . . . no window . . . no hidden entrance.
It was impossible to climb up the outside for
the sides were so smooth there was neither
crack nor ledge where he could put his feet.
In the end the disappointed Prince had to give
up his quest and ride home with the sound of
the voice drifting in the wind behind him.

The Prince could not forget the voice. He dreamed about it in daydreams and dreamed about it in his sleep. He rode into the forest every day, just to hear it.

One day, when he was sitting in the branches of the tree closest to the tower, an old witch came out of the forest. The Prince kept very quiet and watched to see what she would do.

She went to the foot of the tower, and called,

"Rapunzel, Rapunzel, let down your hair."

Immediately, a long braid of golden hair tumbled from the window at the top of the tower. It was so long, its tip touched the ground. The old witch caught hold of it as though it was a rope and someone, in the room at the top of the tower, pulled her upwards until she disappeared.

The Prince was so excited he almost fell out of the tree. He waited until the old witch had come down again and hobbled away into the forest, then he went to the foot of the tower himself.

"Rapunzel, Rapunzel," he called. "Let down your hair."

Again the golden hair came tumbling from the tower, but this time it was a handsome prince who used it as a rope and not an ugly old witch. In the tiny room at the top of the tower was the most beautiful girl he had ever seen.

"Who . . . who . . . are you?" she gasped as he climbed over the windowsill and into the room. "I thought you were the witch."

"Do not be afraid," said the Prince, "I will not hurt you."

He told her his name and how he had heard her singing when he was riding in the forest.

"I sing because I am lonely," said Rapunzel. "I have been locked alone in this tower since I was twelve years old. My only visitor is the witch who brought me here."

"I will help you escape," said the Prince.

"How can you?" sighed Rapunzel. "I cannot climb down my own hair and there is no other way in, or out of, the tower."

"I will bring you a silken ladder," promised the Prince.

That evening the old witch visited Rapunzel again.

"You are much heavier than the Prince," said Rapunzel, without thinking of the consequences of her words. "Why is that?"

The witch was so angry she almost exploded. She had locked Rapunzel in the tower to keep her away from handsome princes. She wanted Rapunzel to love no one in the world but herself. She snatched a pair of scissors from the table, and before Rapunzel could stop her she had cut off her long braids of golden hair.

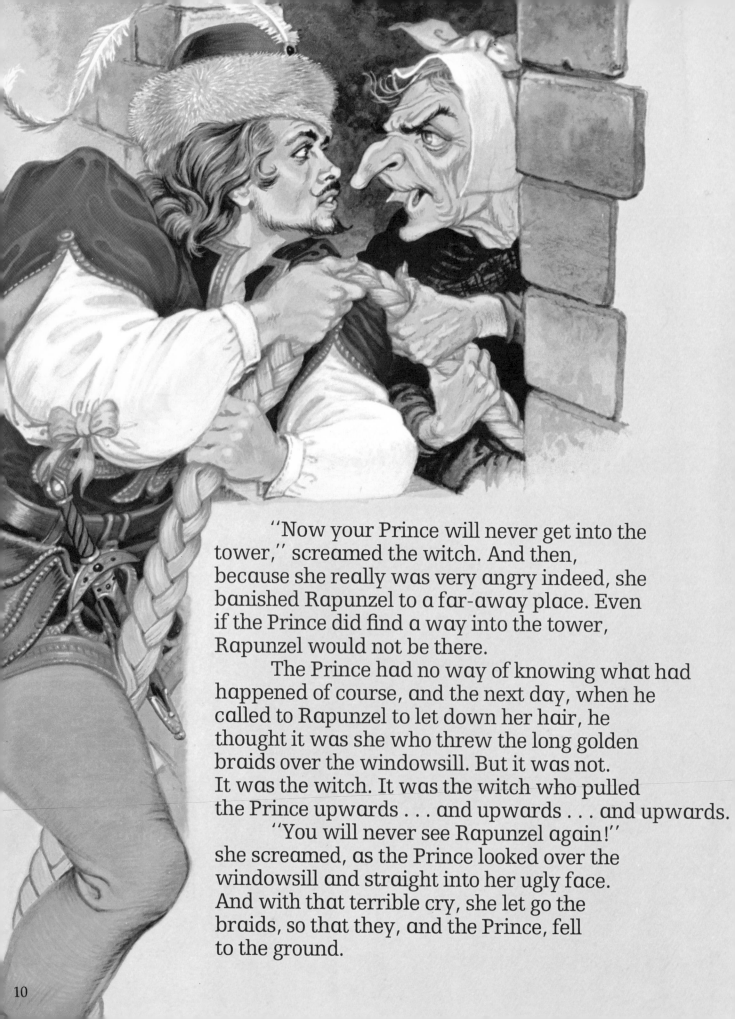

"Now your Prince will never get into the tower," screamed the witch. And then, because she really was very angry indeed, she banished Rapunzel to a far-away place. Even if the Prince did find a way into the tower, Rapunzel would not be there.

The Prince had no way of knowing what had happened of course, and the next day, when he called to Rapunzel to let down her hair, he thought it was she who threw the long golden braids over the windowsill. But it was not. It was the witch. It was the witch who pulled the Prince upwards . . . and upwards . . . and upwards.

"You will never see Rapunzel again!" she screamed, as the Prince looked over the windowsill and straight into her ugly face. And with that terrible cry, she let go the braids, so that they, and the Prince, fell to the ground.

The Prince was bumped and bruised, and when at last he stirred, and opened his eyes, he could not see. He was blind.

The Prince thought Rapunzel was locked in the tower with the witch and though he tried, he could find no way of helping her. He wandered about the countryside, blind, lonely and unhappy.

And then one day, just by chance, he came to the place where Rapunzel was living. He heard her singing and, though her voice was as sad as a flower without petals, he recognized it at once.

"Rapunzel," he called softly. "Is that you?"

Rapunzel was overjoyed, but when she saw the Prince's poor blind eyes, she wept hot, splashing tears. Some of her tears fell onto the Prince's face. Suddenly he could see. Her tears had broken the witch's terrible spell.

Rapunzel and the Prince were married and lived happily ever after. And as for the old witch, she was never heard of, or seen again. Perhaps she is still locked in the tower. Once she had let go of the braids she had no way of getting out of the tower herself, had she?

Twelve Dancing Princesses

Once upon a time, there was a King who had twelve beautiful daughters, and an unusual problem. Every night, when the twelve princesses were sent to bed their shoes were perfectly sound. Every morning when they came down to breakfast their shoes were full of holes. Every day the King had to buy twelve pairs of new shoes. That was expensive, though the expense did not worry the King. What did worry him was not knowing WHY the shoes were full of holes.

He tried locking the bedroom door on the outside when all the princesses were safely inside, and sleeping with the key under his pillow. It made no difference. The princesses' shoes were still full of holes in the morning.

The King was so puzzled, and so vexed, because he couldn't find out WHY it was happening that he issued a proclamation.

It said, WHOMSOEVER SHALL DISCOVER WHY THE PRINCESSES' SHOES ARE FULL OF HOLES EVERY MORNING SHALL HAVE ONE OF THE PRINCESSES FOR HIS WIFE AND SHALL INHERIT MY KINGDOM WHEN I DIE.

Princes came from far and wide to try to find an answer to the mystery. Not one of them succeeded. The puzzled King was beginning to despair of ever finding an answer when a poor soldier came to the palace. The proclamation had said nothing about being a prince if you wanted to solve the mystery, so he had decided to make an attempt at it himself.

The King received the soldier as kindly, and as grandly, as any of the Princes, and that night he was taken to a room adjoining the princesses' bedroom so that he could keep watch.

Now it so happened, that the soldier had been kind to a wise old woman on his way to the palace, and she had given him a cloak, and some advice. "When the princesses offer you wine," she had said, "pretend to drink it and then pretend to fall asleep. Wear the cloak when you want to be invisible."

That night, when the princesses were ready for bed, the eldest said to the soldier,

"You must be thirsty. Take this cup of wine and drink."

The soldier remembered the wise woman's words and pretended to drink. And then, he pretended to get drowsy. Presently he closed his eyes as though he was asleep.

As soon as they heard him snore the princesses jumped from their beds and put on their shoes and their prettiest dresses.

"Are you all ready?" asked the eldest.

"We are ready," replied her sisters.

The eldest princess pressed a carved leaf on the end of her bed. The bed moved slowly to one side and revealed a hidden staircase leading down into the earth. The princesses picked up their skirts and hurried down the steps, the eldest leading the way, and the youngest following last of all.

The soldier, who of course was awake and had seen everything,
put the cloak the old woman had given him round his shoulders.
It covered him from head to toe and made him completely invisible.

He ran after the princesses and caught up with them at the
bottom of the steps. He was in such a hurry not to be left
behind that he accidentally stepped on the hem of the youngest
princess's dress, and tore it.

"Oh . . ." she gasped. "Someone has stepped on my dress."

"Don't be silly," said her sisters. "You caught it on a
nail . . . come hurry . . . we must not be late."

At the bottom of the steps there was a wood in which all the
trees had silver leaves. The soldier broke off one, and put it
in his pocket.

"What was that?" cried the youngest princess in alarm, as she heard the snap of the breaking twig.

"It was nothing . . ." said her sisters.

Next, they passed through an avenue in which all the trees had golden leaves. Again the princess heard the snap of a breaking twig, but again her sisters told her it was her own imagination playing tricks on her.

The running princesses came to the shores of a wide blue lake. At the edge of the lake were twelve boats, with twelve handsome princes sitting, waiting, at the oars. The soldier sat in the boat which was to carry the youngest princess.

"I wonder what makes the boat so heavy today," said the prince, as he pulled, harder than usual, at the oars.

On the far side of the lake there was a magnificent palace from which the sounds of music and merry-making came . . . and it was there that the mystery of the worn out shoes was solved. The twelve princesses danced the entire night with the twelve handsome princes.

Just before dawn, and when all their shoes were in shreds, the princes rowed the princesses back across the lake, and the princesses ran home.

As soon as they reached their bedroom they hurried to look at the soldier. He had run home ahead of them and they found him on his bed, still sleeping, or so they thought.

"We are safe . . ." said the eldest princess.

The soldier followed the princesses to the secret palace the next night, and the following night too. On the third night he took the jewelled cup from which the youngest princess drank and slipped it into a pocket in the invisible cloak.

On the morning after the third night, the King sent for the soldier, and said,

"Your time is up. Either tell me why my daughters' shoes are worn through every morning, or be banished forever . . ."

"Your daughters' shoes are worn because they dance every night in an underground palace," said the soldier, and he told the King all that he had seen.

The princesses gasped and turned pale as the soldier took the silver leaf, the golden leaf, and the jewelled cup from his pocket and handed them to the King. They knew now they could not deny that what the soldier said was true.

"We must confess," said the eldest princess.

The King was so relieved to have the mystery of the worn shoes explained, he couldn't stay cross with his daughters for long.

"Now I shall be able to sleep at night," he said.

The King kept the promise he had made in the proclamation, and the soldier married the princess of his choice. And many years later, when the old King died, he became King in his place.

The Three Spinners

Once there was a girl who could not spin thread. She could do other things, but she could not, or would not, spin. It made her mother very angry to see her sitting idle at the spinning wheel.

"You lazy, lazy girl," she would shout, and then she would hit the girl across the shoulders.

One day, when she was shouting, and the girl was sitting crying at the spinning wheel, the Queen happened to pass by in her coach. She heard the girl crying and called to her coachman to stop the horses.

"Why are you beating your daughter?" she asked. "Why are you shouting at her? Why is she crying? What has she done?"

A Queen's questions should always be answered truthfully, but the old woman was too ashamed to say she thought her daughter was lazy, so she said instead,

"My daughter loves to spin. I am only a poor old woman and I cannot afford to buy the flax. She cries because she wants to spin . . . I do not know what to do."

"Your troubles are over," said the Queen, who as it happened, loved to hear the whirr of the spinning wheel and to see freshly spun thread. "I have plenty of flax at the palace. I will take your daughter home with me and she can spin as much as she likes."

The Queen took the girl to the palace and showed her three rooms which were full from floor to ceiling with unspun flax.

"Spin all THAT flax into thread, my dear, and you shall marry my son," said the Queen.

The poor girl did not know what to do. Of course she wanted to marry the prince, but how could she? She didn't know HOW to spin. For three whole days she sat and wept. On the third day the Queen came to see her.

"Why are you weeping child? Why haven't you started to spin?" asked the Queen.

The poor girl sobbed even harder.

"I brought you to the palace to spin flax," said the Queen sternly. "If there is no thread for me to see tomorrow you will be punished."

When the Queen had swept majestically from the room, the poor, sad girl stood at the window overlooking the street and cried as though her heart would break. Presently, through her tears, she saw three strange women walking along the pavement. One of them had a very broad, flat foot. One had a lip that hung down over her chin, and the third had an enormous thumb.

One of the women called up to the window and asked the girl why she was weeping.

"I do so want to marry the prince," she sobbed, "But first I must spin all this flax, and I do not know how to spin."

"If you will call us aunt and be unashamed of our strange appearance, and if you will invite us to sit with you at your wedding, we will help you," said the three women.

"I shall be glad to call you aunt," said the girl.

The three strange women were as good as their word. They slipped unnoticed into the palace and set to work. The one with the broad, flat foot worked the spinning wheel. The one with the lip which hung over her chin wetted the flax. And the one with the enormous thumb twisted the thread. Together they spun the finest thread the Queen had ever seen. She was impressed, though she thought the girl herself had done the spinning for the three strange women hid whenever they heard the Queen coming.

At last all the flax had been spun and it was time for the wedding. When the arrangements were being made, the girl said to the Queen,

"I have three aunts who have been very kind to me. May I invite them to the wedding and may they sit with me at the table?"

"Of course," said the Queen.

An invitation was sent, and on the day of the wedding the three strange women arrived and were welcomed kindly by the girl and the Prince.

"Tell me Aunt," said the Prince, who couldn't help noticing such things. "Why have you such a broad flat foot?"

"Because I tread a spinning wheel," said the first aunt.

"And how is it that you have such a long lip?" he asked the second aunt.

"Because I wet the spinning thread."

"And why have you such a large thumb?" asked the Prince of the third aunt.

"Because I twist the spinning thread," she answered.

The Prince looked at the three strange women, one with a broad flat foot, one with a lip that hung down over her chin and one with an enormous thumb, and then he looked at his beautiful bride.

"If that is what spinning thread does to a woman," he said, "I forbid you ever to touch a spinning wheel."

And so the girl married her prince, and the three spinners moved into the palace to take care of all the spinning. They loved spinning as much as the girl loved the prince and so everyone was happy.

Foolish Jack

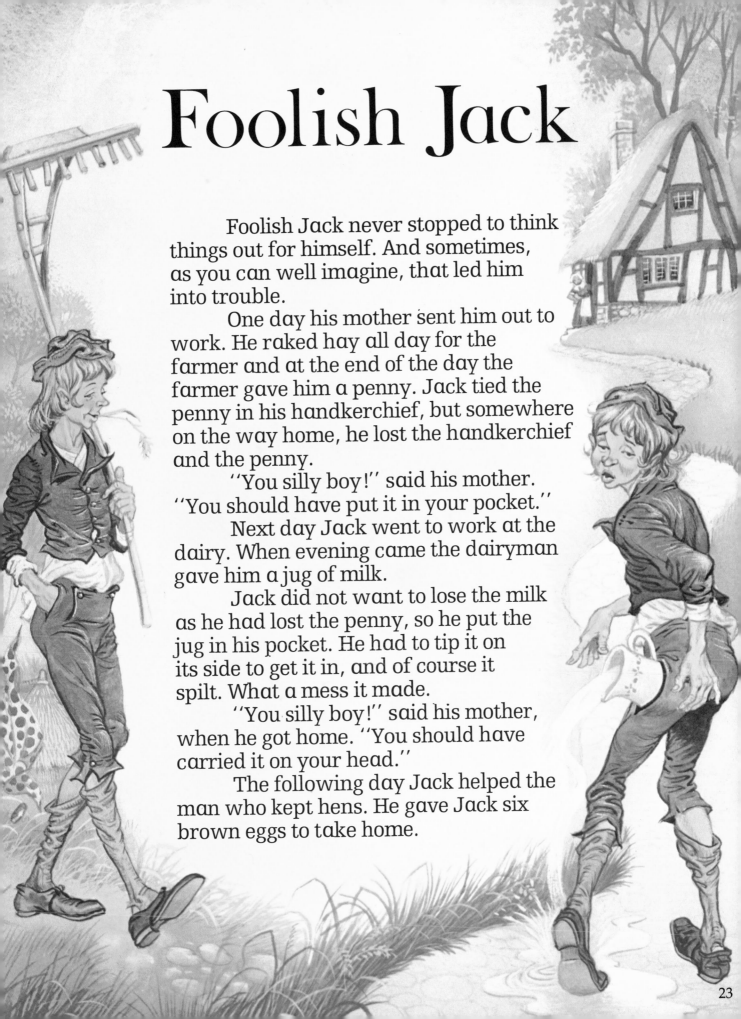

Foolish Jack never stopped to think things out for himself. And sometimes, as you can well imagine, that led him into trouble.

One day his mother sent him out to work. He raked hay all day for the farmer and at the end of the day the farmer gave him a penny. Jack tied the penny in his handkerchief, but somewhere on the way home, he lost the handkerchief and the penny.

''You silly boy!'' said his mother. ''You should have put it in your pocket.''

Next day Jack went to work at the dairy. When evening came the dairyman gave him a jug of milk.

Jack did not want to lose the milk as he had lost the penny, so he put the jug in his pocket. He had to tip it on its side to get it in, and of course it spilt. What a mess it made.

''You silly boy!'' said his mother, when he got home. ''You should have carried it on your head.''

The following day Jack helped the man who kept hens. He gave Jack six brown eggs to take home.

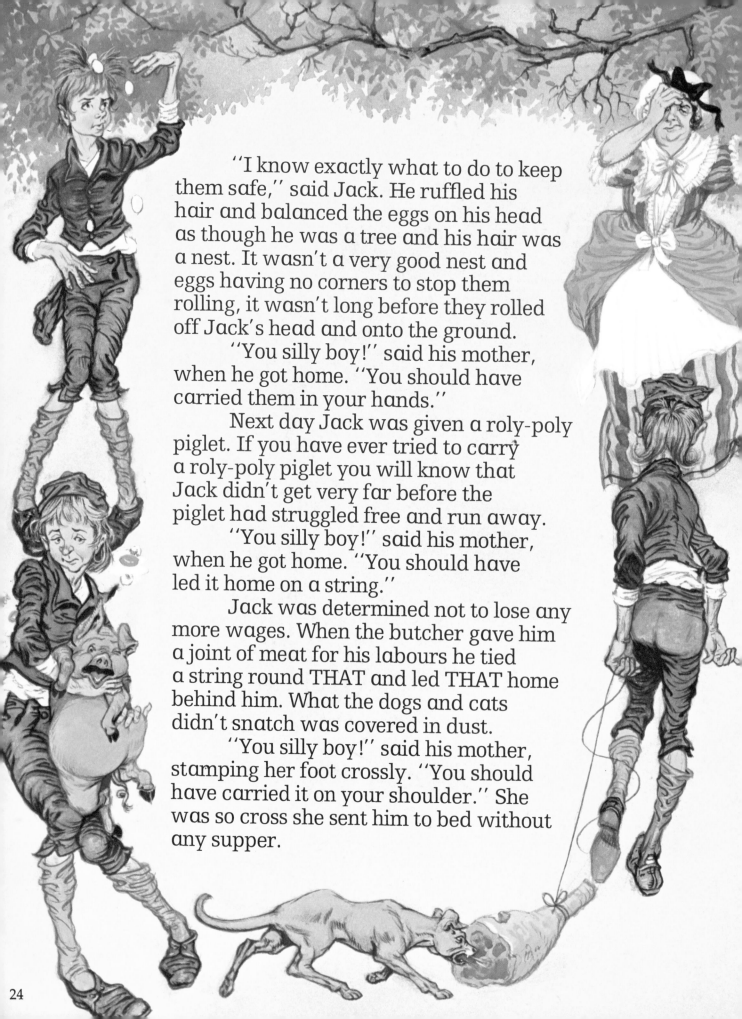

"I know exactly what to do to keep them safe," said Jack. He ruffled his hair and balanced the eggs on his head as though he was a tree and his hair was a nest. It wasn't a very good nest and eggs having no corners to stop them rolling, it wasn't long before they rolled off Jack's head and onto the ground.

"You silly boy!" said his mother, when he got home. "You should have carried them in your hands."

Next day Jack was given a roly-poly piglet. If you have ever tried to carry a roly-poly piglet you will know that Jack didn't get very far before the piglet had struggled free and run away.

"You silly boy!" said his mother, when he got home. "You should have led it home on a string."

Jack was determined not to lose any more wages. When the butcher gave him a joint of meat for his labours he tied a string round THAT and led THAT home behind him. What the dogs and cats didn't snatch was covered in dust.

"You silly boy!" said his mother, stamping her foot crossly. "You should have carried it on your shoulder." She was so cross she sent him to bed without any supper.

And then Jack's luck changed, though
it didn't seem like it to begin with.
He had worked all day for the goatherd
and had been given a goat to take home.

Now it so happened that on the way
home every day Jack had to pass the house
of a rich man. The rich man had a
beautiful daughter who had never laughed,
and he promised that the first person
to make her laugh should marry her.

She had watched Jack go by the house
every day. When she saw him trying to
carry eggs on his head, her eyes had
twinkled. When she saw him trying to
carry a roly-poly piglet she had smiled,
just a little. On the day he came past
the house with a protesting goat wrapped
round his neck like a scarf and with his
own knees buckling beneath him, she burst
into merry peals of laughter.

And that was how Jack found a wife.
She was as sensible as she was rich, and
she taught Jack how to think for himself,
and so they lived happily ever after.

The Precious Gift

Once upon a time, there was a King who had three daughters. One day, one of them would be queen. The King could not decide which of them it should be, for they were all beautiful and they were all clever.

"I must make up my mind somehow," he said. "I wonder what I can do?" He thought, and he thought, and at last he made a decision. "I will ask each of my daughters to bring me a gift," he said, "and the one who brings the most precious shall be queen."

On the appointed day he summoned them to the throne room.

The eldest brought a silver bird in a silver cage, which sang when a key was wound.

"A truly beautiful gift," murmured the King.

The second daughter brought a robe of finest silk, trimmed with the softest fur.

"Another truly beautiful gift," murmured the King.

The third daughter brought a plain china bowl which was so small it nestled in the palm of her hand. The King held his breath as he lifted the lid. What precious gift would he find inside it? When the King did see what was in the tiny bowl his face went red, and then it went purple.

"How dare you!" he shouted. He jumped to his feet and threw the little bowl to the floor.

"How dare you insult me by bringing me common salt!"

"But . . . but . . ." The poor little princess tried to say something, but the King shouted and the more he shouted the more angry he became.

"Go!" he shouted. "Go! And never come back. Never! Never! NEVER!"

Of course he was sorry he had said what he did when his temper cooled down, but by then it was too late. The little princess had left the palace.

She wandered sadly until she came to an inn.

"Please let me stay here," she begged. "I have nowhere to go. I will work. I will do anything you ask."

The innkeeper did not know she was a princess or he would have given her his best room and waited on her himself. Instead he sent her down to the kitchen to help the cook.

The cook was a kindly woman. She taught the little princess all she knew about cooking. The princess was quick to learn and before long people were coming to the inn specially to taste her pies and to sample her soups and sauces. The kindly old cook was getting old and gradually the little princess did more and more of the cooking, until soon, she was doing it all.

Everyone who went to the inn talked for days afterwards about the delicious food eaten there, and it was only a matter of time before the King came to hear about the cook who could cook anything, and what was more, cook it perfectly.

"She must come to work in the palace kitchens," he said. "She is the best, and the King always has the best."

And so it was, that the King's own daughter, worked in the palace kitchens and cooked the King's meals, and no one, least of all the King, had any idea who she really was.

The day came when the King's eldest daughter was to be married. Such a hustle and a bustle there was in the palace kitchens. Any banquet is important, but a wedding banquet is the most important of all, especially when a princess is marrying a prince. The little princess, who was now a cook, worked hard and long to get everything prepared.

After the wedding the King and his guests sat down at the tables in the banqueting hall. The King clapped his hands.

"Let the banquet and the merry-making begin," he cried.

The pages and the footmen filed into the hall carrying silver platters piled high with the most delicious food it had ever been the King's privilege to see.

"What a wonderful cook you must have," said a visiting emperor.

The King felt so proud. And then, as was the custom, he lifted his fork and took the first bite of food. Everyone watched, and waited for the sign that they too could begin to eat. To their astonishment the King pulled a face and spat out the food.

Princes and princesses, lords and ladies, footmen and pages, stared at the King with open mouths as he tried dish, after dish, scowling harder and harder with each mouthful he tasted. Suddenly he threw down his fork and in a voice like thunder, he shouted,

"FETCH THE COOK!"

He looked so angry everyone trembled, even the visiting emperor, and he didn't frighten easily.

29

"What's wrong?...what's wrong?..." echoed in whispers round the hall.

The cook came and stood, with her head bowed, in front of the King, who by now was scarlet with rage.

"You have cooked the food without salt!" he roared. "The banquet is ruined! You have shamed me in front of my guests! How dare you forget something so important!"

"But I did not forget," said the cook, who was really a princess. The King was so astonished at a humble cook daring to answer him back he said nothing, and so she was able to continue.

"A long time ago, you banished a daughter because she gave you a gift of common salt..."

The King sat down with a bump on his chair. Yes, he did remember that. He had been sorry ever since. But how did the cook know about it? He looked at her closely. She lifted her head so that he could see her face, and smiled. The King jumped to his feet, scattering dishes with a clatter he did not hear.

"Daughter..." he cried. "It's you! Can you ever forgive me? You truly gave me a very precious gift and I was too foolish to know it."

Of course the princess forgave her father. And the banquet was not spoilt because she had arranged that only the King's food should be cooked without salt. There was more food already prepared for him in the kitchen.

And so the King and his daughter were reunited and the princess once again took her rightful place in the palace.

The Ugly Duckling

Once, somewhere in the country, there was a duck who had a clutch of eggs to hatch. Five of them hatched into fluffy little ducklings, but the sixth, which for some reason was bigger than all the others, lay in the nest, smooth and unbroken.

"That's much too big to be a duck egg," said one of the duck's friends. "Looks more like a turkey egg to me."

"How will I be able to tell?" asked the duck.

"It will not swim when it is hatched," said her friend. "Turkeys never do."

But the egg wasn't a turkey egg because the bird that hatched from it DID swim. It swam as well as any duckling.

"That last duckling of yours is very ugly," laughed the farmyard hens. It was true. He wasn't a bit like his brothers and sisters.

"What an ugly duckling," laughed the geese when they saw him. And somehow that name stuck. Whenever anyone wanted him they called, "Ugly duckling, where are you?" or if they didn't want him they said, "Ugly duckling, go away." He even thought of himself as ugly duckling. He was very sad. He didn't like being ugly. He didn't like being teased. No one would play with him. No one would swim with him. Even his mother made fun of him. One day, the ugly duckling ran away. And I am sorry to say, no one missed him at all.

The ugly duckling hoped he would find someone in the big wide world, to be his friend. Someone who wouldn't mind how ugly he was. But the wild ducks were just as unkind as the farmyard ducks, and the wild geese honked at him and made fun, just as the farmyard geese had done.

"Am I never to find a friend? Am I never to be happy?" sighed the ugly duckling.

One day, as he sat alone and unhappy in the middle of a lake on the bleak flat marshes, he heard the steady beat of wings. When he looked up there were swans flying overhead with their long necks stretched before them and their white feathers gleaming in the sun. They were so beautiful. If only he had been born a swan. But he hadn't. He had been born a duckling and an ugly one at that.

The ugly duckling stayed on the lake all through the long hard winter. Food was hard to find and he was often hungry. Once he was trapped in some ice and thought he would die. He was set free, just in time, by a farmer and his dog.

Spring came and the lake where he had spent the lonely winter became a busy, exciting, and noisy place. The ducks were forever quacking and the geese were forever honking. There was plenty of splashing and excitement. But not for the ugly duckling. No one quacked the latest piece of gossip to him. Sadly he spread his wings and took to the sky. He had never flown before and he was surprised how strong his wings were. They carried him away from the lake and the marshes and over a leafy garden.

On a still, clear pond in the garden, he could see the beautiful white swans, with their gracefully arched necks, and suddenly the ugly duckling felt that he did not want to live any longer.

"I will go down to the pond and ask those beautiful birds to kill me," he said. And down he went to the water. He bent his head humbly and closed his eyes.

"Kill me," he said to the swans. "I am too ugly to live."

"Ugly?" said the swans. "Have you looked at your reflection?"

"I do not need to look. I know how ugly I am," said the ugly duckling.

"Look into the water." said the swans. And so the ugly duckling did. What he saw made his heart beat fast and filled him with happiness. During the long winter months he had changed.

"I'm . . . I'm just like you . . ." he whispered.

When the children who lived in the garden came to feed the swans they called to one another,

"A new swan . . . a new swan . . . isn't he beautiful?" And then the ugly duckling knew without a doubt that he really WAS a swan, that he had ALWAYS been a swan and that his days of being lonely were over.

The Brave Little Tailor

One day, a tailor was sitting at his bench sewing a seam with his needle and thread. Beside him was a plate and on the plate was a slice of bread and jam. It was his lunch and the sooner he finished sewing the seam the sooner he could eat it. He liked jam spread on bread. He wasn't the only one.

"Jam . . ." buzzed the greedy flies. "We smell jam."

"Don't you dare!" shouted the little tailor. He picked up a piece of cloth. "Take that!" he shouted, and he swatted at the flies as hard as he could. Seven of them fell dead to the table.

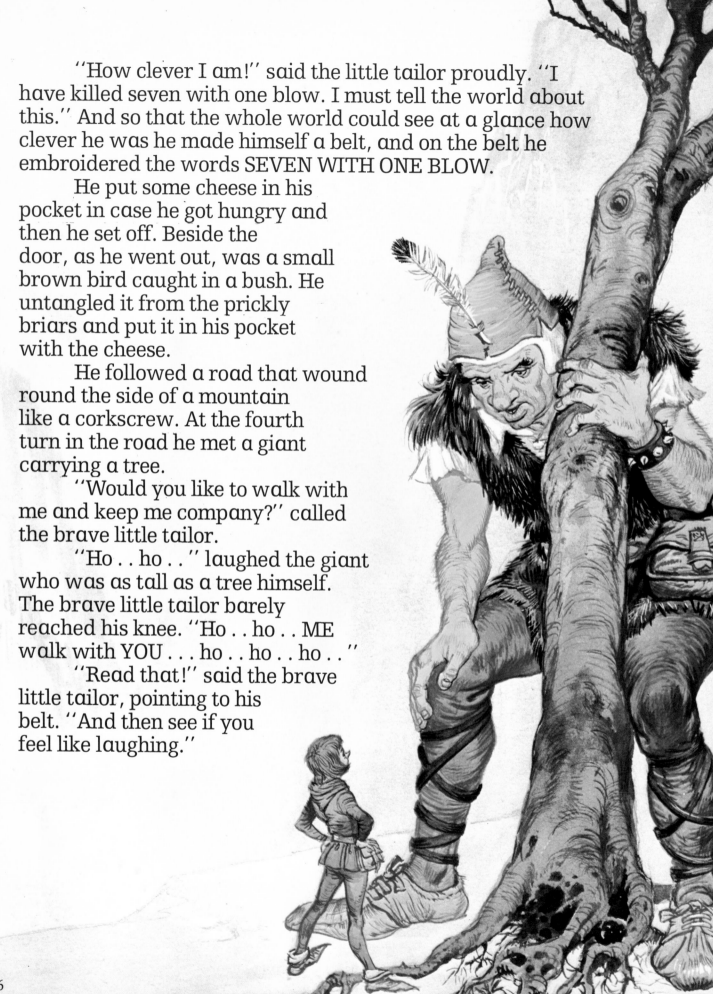

"How clever I am!" said the little tailor proudly. "I have killed seven with one blow. I must tell the world about this." And so that the whole world could see at a glance how clever he was he made himself a belt, and on the belt he embroidered the words SEVEN WITH ONE BLOW.

He put some cheese in his pocket in case he got hungry and then he set off. Beside the door, as he went out, was a small brown bird caught in a bush. He untangled it from the prickly briars and put it in his pocket with the cheese.

He followed a road that wound round the side of a mountain like a corkscrew. At the fourth turn in the road he met a giant carrying a tree.

"Would you like to walk with me and keep me company?" called the brave little tailor.

"Ho . . ho . ." laughed the giant who was as tall as a tree himself. The brave little tailor barely reached his knee. "Ho . . ho . . ME walk with YOU . . . ho . . ho . . ho . ."

"Read that!" said the brave little tailor, pointing to his belt. "And then see if you feel like laughing."

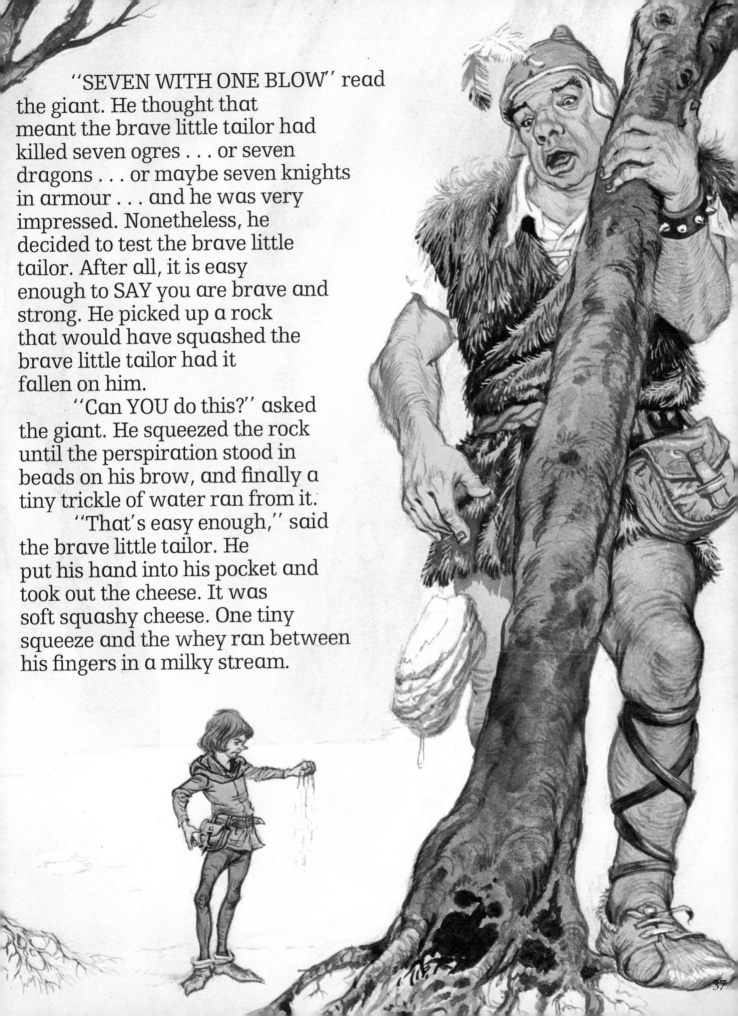

"SEVEN WITH ONE BLOW" read the giant. He thought that meant the brave little tailor had killed seven ogres . . . or seven dragons . . . or maybe seven knights in armour . . . and he was very impressed. Nonetheless, he decided to test the brave little tailor. After all, it is easy enough to SAY you are brave and strong. He picked up a rock that would have squashed the brave little tailor had it fallen on him.

"Can YOU do this?" asked the giant. He squeezed the rock until the perspiration stood in beads on his brow, and finally a tiny trickle of water ran from it.

"That's easy enough," said the brave little tailor. He put his hand into his pocket and took out the cheese. It was soft squashy cheese. One tiny squeeze and the whey ran between his fingers in a milky stream.

"Oh!" said the giant, rather taken aback. Then he said, "Can YOU throw as far as this?" He picked up a small boulder and hurled it with all his might. It flew through the air like a thunderbolt and landed with a thud on the grass, at least half a league away.

"Easily," said the brave little tailor. This time he took the little brown bird from his pocket. It had got over its fright at being tangled in the briar and was glad to be free. When the brave little tailor tossed it into the air, it flew and flew until it was just a tiny speck in the distance.

"It will fall to the ground sooner or later," said the brave little tailor. "Probably later, rather than sooner."

"If you're THAT strong," said the giant, feeling more than a little put out, "you can help me carry this tree home."

"Glad to," said the brave little tailor. "You go in front and take the roots, I'll follow behind and carry the branches, which are the heaviest part."

The giant lifted the heavy trunk back onto his shoulder. The knobbly roots stuck out in front of him like a lopsided beard and he didn't see the brave little tailor leap nimbly into the branches behind him and settle himself comfortably.

"Ready when you are!" called the brave little tailor.

He rode all the way to the giant's cave. His feet didn't touch the ground once. When they got to the cave the giant lowered the tree to the ground and sat down himself. He didn't see the brave little tailor jump to the ground. The brave little tailor wasn't the slightest bit out of breath. He didn't look the slightest bit tired. The giant couldn't believe his eyes. HE was tired. HE was out of breath. And he was frightened as well. If the brave little tailor was as strong as he seemed to be then he could be dangerous, even to a giant. He would have to be got rid of.

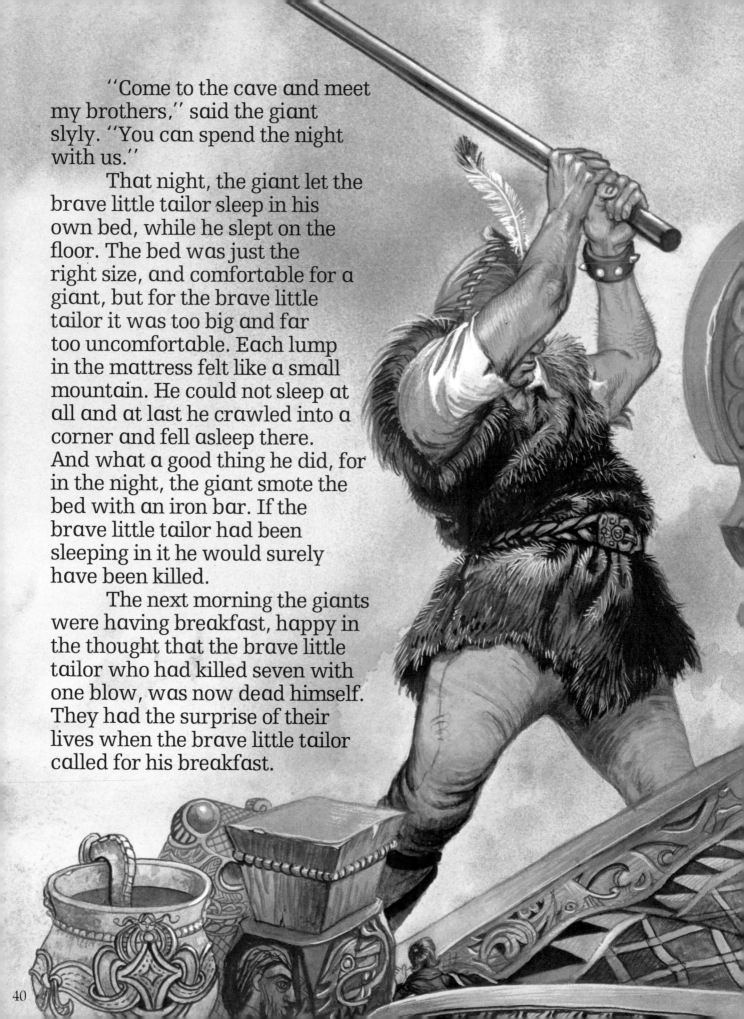

"Come to the cave and meet my brothers," said the giant slyly. "You can spend the night with us."

That night, the giant let the brave little tailor sleep in his own bed, while he slept on the floor. The bed was just the right size, and comfortable for a giant, but for the brave little tailor it was too big and far too uncomfortable. Each lump in the mattress felt like a small mountain. He could not sleep at all and at last he crawled into a corner and fell asleep there. And what a good thing he did, for in the night, the giant smote the bed with an iron bar. If the brave little tailor had been sleeping in it he would surely have been killed.

The next morning the giants were having breakfast, happy in the thought that the brave little tailor who had killed seven with one blow, was now dead himself. They had the surprise of their lives when the brave little tailor called for his breakfast.

They bellowed with fright and ran from the cave. They ran until they came to the sea and they splashed through that until they reached the land on the far side. They are probably running still. The brave little tailor puffed out his chest when he saw the three giants running away from HIM. He felt brave enough to conquer a hundred giants.

He tricked a lot of people into believing he was stronger than he really was. Even kings trembled at the thought of what he might do. One day he became a king himself, but that is a story for another time.

The Pedlar of Swaffham

Once, long ago, when London Bridge was lined with shops, a pedlar living in the country, far away from London, had a strange dream. He dreamed that if he went to London Bridge he would hear some good news. The first time he had the dream he didn't take much notice of it. The second time he had the dream he began to wonder, and the third time he had the dream, he decided to make the trip to London Town.

He was too poor to hire a horse and it was a very long walk. His shoes had almost worn out by the time he got there.

He walked up and down the bridge for three days waiting to hear what the good news might be. On the third day, one of the shopkeepers who kept a shop on the bridge could bear it no longer. He left his wife to serve the customers and went to speak to the pedlar.

"I've watched you walk up and down for three whole days," he said. "Have you something to sell?"

"No," said the pedlar.

"Then are you begging?" asked the shopkeeper, looking at his worn shoes and dusty coat.

"Certainly not," said the pedlar.

"Then what ARE you doing?" asked the shopkeeper.

The pedlar told him about his dream.

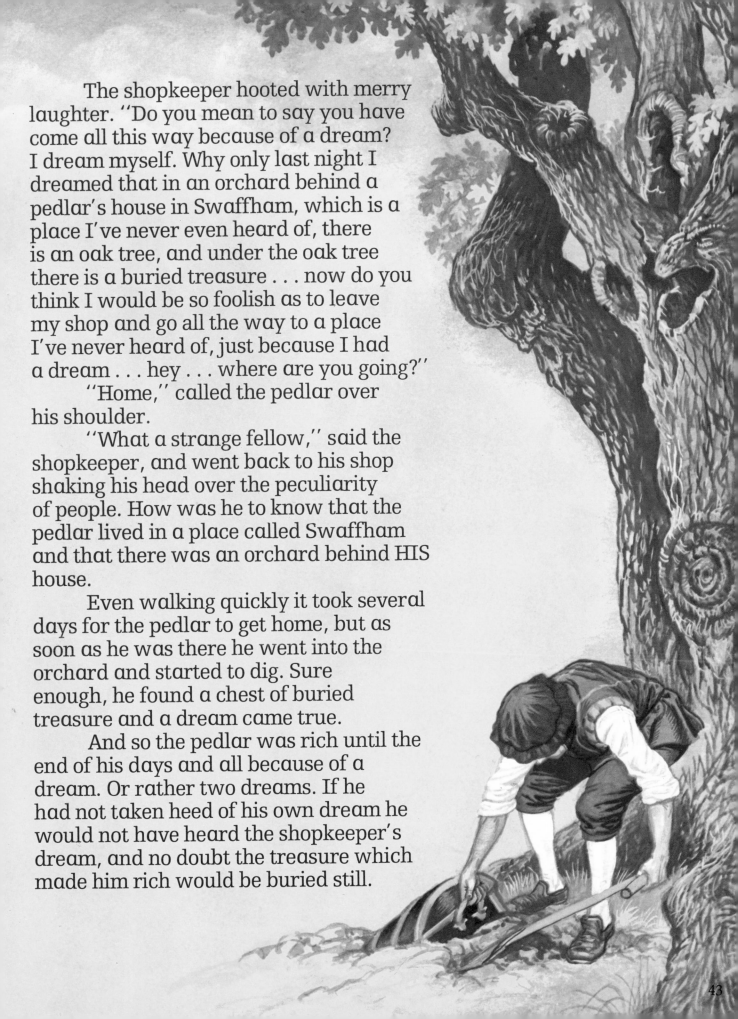

The shopkeeper hooted with merry laughter. "Do you mean to say you have come all this way because of a dream? I dream myself. Why only last night I dreamed that in an orchard behind a pedlar's house in Swaffham, which is a place I've never even heard of, there is an oak tree, and under the oak tree there is a buried treasure . . . now do you think I would be so foolish as to leave my shop and go all the way to a place I've never heard of, just because I had a dream . . . hey . . . where are you going?"

"Home," called the pedlar over his shoulder.

"What a strange fellow," said the shopkeeper, and went back to his shop shaking his head over the peculiarity of people. How was he to know that the pedlar lived in a place called Swaffham and that there was an orchard behind HIS house.

Even walking quickly it took several days for the pedlar to get home, but as soon as he was there he went into the orchard and started to dig. Sure enough, he found a chest of buried treasure and a dream came true.

And so the pedlar was rich until the end of his days and all because of a dream. Or rather two dreams. If he had not taken heed of his own dream he would not have heard the shopkeeper's dream, and no doubt the treasure which made him rich would be buried still.

Puss in Boots

Once upon a time, there was a miller, who had three sons. When he died he left his mill to his first son, his donkey to his second son, and because he had nothing else, he left his cat to his third son.

The first son ground flour at the mill and sold it. The second son harnessed the donkey to a cart and carried things for paying customers. But what could the third son do with a cat, except let him sit in the sun, and purr, and drink milk?

One day, the cat said,

"Master, give me a pair of boots and a sack and you will see that I am not as useless as you think." It was a very strange request for a cat to make, but it was granted nonetheless.

The cat, or Puss in Boots, as the miller's son now called him, went into the forest and caught a rabbit. He put it in the sack and then instead of taking it home to the miller's son, he took it to the King's palace.

"Please accept this small present from my master the Marquis of Carabas," said Puss in Boots.

It was to be the first of many presents Puss in Boots took to the King, and each time he said he had been sent by his master the Marquis of Carabas. And though the King never actually met the Marquis of Carabas, he soon became very familiar with his name. The miller's son knew nothing of the presents, or of the Marquis of Carabas, and Puss in Boots didn't tell him.

One day, when Puss in Boots was at the palace, he overheard someone say that the King was about to take his daughter for a drive in the country. Puss in Boots hurried home.

"Quick master!" he called. "Go and bathe in the river and I will make your fortune."

It was another strange request for a cat to make but the miller's son was used to his pet by now and so he did as he was told. No sooner was he in the river than Puss in Boots took his clothes and threw them into the river with him.

"Puss . . . Puss . . . what are you doing?" called the miller's son.

Puss didn't answer, he was watching the road. Presently he saw the King's carriage in the distance. He waited until it was close then he ran out in the road in front of it.

"Help! Help! My master the Marquis of Carabas is drowning! Please save him!"

45

It took but a moment to drag the miller's son, who hadn't the slightest idea what Puss in Boots was up to, from the river and find him some dry clothes. He looked so handsome in the fine velvet tunic and the doublet and hose borrowed from one of the footmen that the princess fell in love with him at once.

"Father dear, may the Marquis of Carabas ride with us?"

The King liked to please his daughter and agreed to her request at once.

"Will you ride with us Puss?" asked the King.

Puss asked to be excused. He said he had something rather important to attend to. He ran on ahead of the carriage, and each time he saw someone at work in the fields he called,

"If the King asks who this land belongs to, tell him it belongs to the Marquis of Carabas."

The King did stop the carriage several times, and each time he received the same answer to his question.

'The Marquis of Carabas must be a very rich man,' he thought.

Puss in Boots ran so swiftly that soon he was a long way ahead of the carriage. Presently he came to a rich and imposing looking castle, which he knew belonged to a cruel and wicked ogre. He went straight up to the ogre without so much as a twitching of a whisker, and said,

"I hear you can turn yourself into any animal you choose. I won't believe a story like that unless I see it for myself."

Immediately, the ogre changed himself into a lion, and roared and growled and snarled.

"There . . ." he said, when he had turned himself back into an ogre. "I hope I frightened you."

"Must be easy to change your-self into something big," said Puss in Boots with a shrug. "I don't suppose you can turn your-self into something as small as a . . . er . . . um . . ." He seemed to be thinking. " . . . er . . . um . . . a mouse?"

The ogre couldn't have a mere cat doubting his special abilities. He changed himself into a tiny mouse in the twinkling of an eye. It was the last time he changed himself into anything because Puss in Boots pounced on him and ate him up before he could change back into an ogre, and THAT was the end of him!

"Hoorah!" shouted the castle servants. "We are free of the wicked ogre at last. Hoorah!"

"Your new master will always be kind, you can be sure of that," said Puss in Boots.

"Who IS our new master?" they asked.

"The Marquis of Carabas of course," said Puss.

When the King's carriage reached the castle, Puss in Boots was standing at the drawbridge, with the smiling servants gathered round him.

"Welcome . ." he said with a beautiful bow. "Welcome to the home of my master the Marquis of Carabas." The miller's son was too astonished to do anything except think to himself,

'Whatever is Puss up to?'

Luckily Puss had time to explain while the King was getting out of the carriage.

'What a rich man this Marquis must be,' thought the King. 'And such a nice young man too.'

Not long afterwards the princess and the miller's son were married. They, and Puss in Boots, lived happily ever after in the castle that had once belonged to the wicked ogre.

The Shepherdess and the Sweep

Once there was a shepherdess. Not a real shepherdess but a delicate porcelain one. She was very beautiful. She stood beside the porcelain sweep, on a table, in a dark and crowded parlour. The sweep was as black as coal, except for his face which was as pink and as clean as the shepherdess's own. Just behind them stood the Chinese mandarin. He had a black stubby pig-tail hanging down his back, and grey slanting eyes. The Chinese mandarin nodded all the time. He couldn't help it. It was the way he was made. The shepherdess called him Grand-father, though he wasn't, because if he had been she would have been Chinese too, and she wasn't.

On the far side of the room and facing the table where the three porcelain figures stood, was a carved wooden cabinet. Carved in the very middle of the door was a very peculiar man. He had a lop-sided smile that was hardly a smile at all, and a beard, and legs like a goat. The children who lived in the house and some-times came into the parlour called him Mr. Goat-legged, Commanding General, Private, Sergeant, because they thought it suited him, though if they were in a hurry they called him Mr. Goat-legs.

One day, Mr. Goat-legs asked the Chinese mandarin if he could marry the shepherdess. The Chinese mandarin nodded, as was his habit.

"Good," said Mr. Goat-legs looking pleased.

"But Grandpa, I don't want to marry horrid Mr. Goat-legs," said the shepherdess.

"It is too late now. I have given my consent," said the Chinese mandarin. "The wedding will be tonight. Wake me up in time for the ceremony." And with no more ado, he nodded himself to sleep.

The little shepherdess cried tears that looked like seed pearls. The sweep tried to comfort her.

"Please take me away from the parlour and out into the wide world," she pleaded. "I cannot marry Mr. Goat-legs."

The running stags carved on the side of the cabinet saw them climbing down to the floor.

"The shepherdess and the sweep are eloping!" they cried.

The mandarin woke with a start and began nodding so furiously, his whole body rocked backwards and forwards. The shepherdess and the sweep had never seen him so angry and were very frightened.

"There is only one way to escape," whispered the sweep. "We must go into the stove and up the chimney to the roof."

It was a difficult climb, even for the sweep. It was dark, and sooty, and steep. The shepherdess was so afraid she would slip. If she fell she knew she would break into a thousand pieces.

"Do not look down," whispered the sweep as he followed behind and guided her feet to the nooks and crannies. "Look up towards the star which shines at the end of our journey."

When the shepherdess looked up through the dark tunnel of the chimney, she could see a tiny speck of light, far, far away in the distance. The higher they climbed the bigger it grew, and when they got to the top it became the entire sky.

The shepherdess and the sweep sat side by side on the rim of the chimney-pot and looked wearily across the rooftops at the wide, wide world. The shepherdess did not like what she saw. The big wide world was so very big, and so very wide. She began to cry again.

"Please take me back to the parlour," she sobbed. "I like the big wide world even less than I like Mr. Goat-legs." Her face was soon stained with sooty tears. The little sweep could not bear to see her so unhappy and agreed to take her back.

The journey down the chimney was just as difficult as the journey up had been. It was just as dark. Just as frightening. When they finally crawled out of the stove and into the parlour they were met by a strange and eerie silence.

"Something has happened!" cried the shepherdess. "Oh I just know something dreadful has happened!"

It had. In his anger, the Chinese mandarin had rolled off the edge of the table and now he was lying in pieces on the floor.

"Oh dear, it's all our fault," cried the shepherdess. "Oh poor Grandpa . . . what are we to do?" And she cried even more.

"We can't do anything," said the sweep, "but don't worry. Someone is sure to come along and glue him together again."

And someone did. But from that day onwards he lost his habit of nodding. It didn't matter how many times Mr. Goat-legs asked if he could still marry the shepherdess, the Chinese mandarin, would not, could not, nod and give his consent. And so the shepherdess and the sweep were able to stand side by side until the end of their days.

The Emperor's New Clothes

Once there was an Emperor who was always changing his clothes. He had a different outfit for every hour of the day. Whenever his ministers wanted him for something special, they always went to the royal clothes closet first. He was more likely to be there deciding what to change into next, than passing laws in his Council Chamber, or balancing the budget in his Counting House.

One day, two men arrived in town. They knew how fond the Emperor was of new clothes and they had hatched a plan. A crafty plan. They spread the news that they could weave the most beautiful cloth anyone had ever seen, and furthermore it was magic, and invisible to anyone who was stupid, or unworthy of the position he held.

"I must have an outfit made from that marvellous new cloth everyone is talking about," said the Emperor, and he sent for the weavers. They agreed to weave some of the cloth for him and went away from the palace carrying silk and golden thread, as well as a large sum of money.

They hid the silk and golden thread in their packs and then set up their loom. There was the steady clack, clack, and the whirr of a busy loom for days. The Emperor was very anxious to see how the new cloth was coming along, but he was just a tiny bit afraid.

'What would I do if I could not see the cloth?' he thought. And though he didn't think for a moment that he wasn't fit to be emperor, he sent his faithful old Prime Minister to look at the cloth in his place.

The weavers led the Prime Minister to their loom. He could not see a single thread.

'Oh dear,' he thought, 'If the Emperor finds out I can't see the cloth I will lose my job. I must pretend I CAN see it.'

''It's the most beautiful piece of cloth in the world,'' he told the Emperor on his return to the palace.

The Emperor decided perhaps he would go and see it for himself after all. He gathered his favourite councillors around him and went to the weavers.

''Show us our beautiful new cloth,'' he said.

''Can you not see it? It's there, on the loom,'' said the weavers.

''So it is . . . so it is . . .'' said the Emperor, his voice full of admiration and his heart full of shame, because HE could not see the cloth either. But then neither could anyone else, though everyone THOUGHT everyone else could see it. There were so many exclamations of delight at the beauty of the new cloth, it really was quite astonishing, in the circumstances.

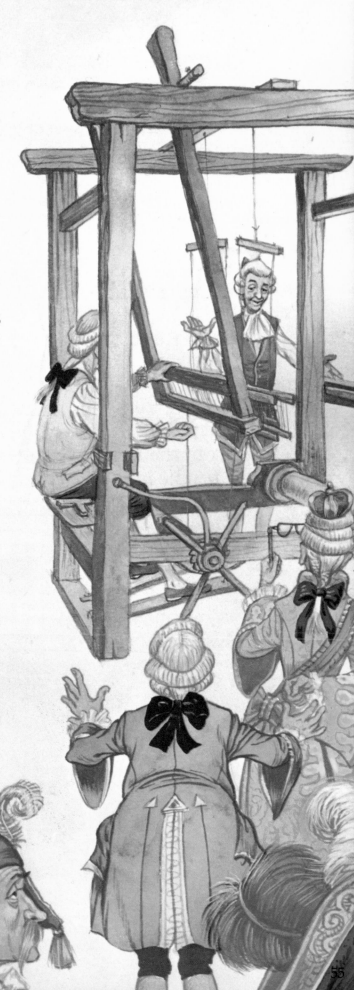

"Make me a suit of clothes from the cloth and I will wear it in procession tomorrow," said the Emperor, outwardly smiling, and inwardly trembling.

The two weavers said they were tailors too, and that they would make the suit themselves. At eight o'clock next morning it was ready. Or so they told the Emperor.

The Emperor bathed. He powdered his hair. He put on his shoes and stockings. And then he let the weavers dress him in the new suit of clothes.

"It's a perfect fit," they said.

"It's a perfect fit," said ALL the councillors.

"It's a perfect fit," said the Emperor, although he could see nothing but his own pink skin.

When the Emperor was ready, or thought he was, the procession through the streets of the town began. Everyone knew about the wonderful cloth. Everyone knew that only those worthy enough could see it, and that to everyone else it was invisible.

"Look at the Emperor's new suit . . . isn't it beautiful . . ?" sighed the people in the crowd as he walked proudly by.

"How well it fits . . ."

"Ahhh . . . truly a suit fit for an emperor . . ."

And then a little voice rang out above the others. It belonged to a boy who never listened to gossip and he hadn't heard the stories about the wonderful cloth, besides his father had taught him always to be truthful.

"The Emperor has no clothes on!" he shouted.

Someone began to laugh. "The boy's right! The Emperor has no clothes on!"

The cry was caught up by the people in the crowd.

"The Emperor has no clothes on . . ."

The poor Emperor was shivering with cold so he knew the crowd must be right, but he walked proudly through the streets and back to the palace with his head held high and his skin blushing a bright and glowing crimson.

He sent guards to fetch the weavers so that they could be punished for daring to trick an emperor, but they had vanished and were never seen again. And from that day onwards, I'm glad to say, the Emperor paid a little less attention to what he wore, and more attention to the affairs of state.

Jorinda and Joringel

Once upon a time, there was a witch who lived in a castle in the middle of a dark and tangled wood. At night she read her magic books, but by day she changed herself into an owl and flew about the wood, ready to cast a spell on anyone who dared to get too close to her castle.

One day a boy and girl were walking in the wood. They had a wedding to plan and a lot to talk about, and they went deeper into the wood than they intended. Just as the sun was about to set, Joringel said,

"We should turn for home . . . we are getting too close to the witch's castle." But it was already too late, for even as he spoke an owl flew from the trees and circled round them.

"Whoo! Whoo! Whoo!" it cried. The witch's spell had been cast. Joringel could not move and Jorinda had been turned into a little brown bird.

The owl flew into the middle of a bush. There was a rustle, and a moment later the old witch herself appeared. She caught the brown bird in a wicker cage and hurried away with it towards the castle. And though Joringel could see everything as it happened, he could do nothing to help Jorinda. He was rooted to the spot. And there he stayed, as still as a stone statue, until the old witch returned and removed the spell.

"Where is Jorinda? What have you done with her? Please bring her back to me," he begged. But the old witch was deaf to all his pleas.

"Go home . . . " she said. "Stop wasting my time."

Joringel tried again, and again, to get into the castle, but every time the witch was ready for him. Whenever he got to within a hundred paces of the grey crumbling walls, she cast her spell afresh, and he could not move. He despaired of ever seeing Jorinda again. And then one night, when he had fallen into an exhausted and fitful sleep, he had a strange dream. He dreamed that he had found a large pearl in the centre of a beautiful red flower. In his dream he picked the flower, and found that everything he touched with it was released from the witch's spell.

When Joringel woke he was determined to search until he found just such a flower. It was the only hope he had. He searched through the woods and the meadows for eight whole days, and then on the ninth day, he found a flower just like the one in his dream, except that instead of a pearl nestling inside its velvety red petals, there was a bright and glistening dew-drop. Joringel picked it carefully so that he did not disturb the dew-drop, then cradled it gently in his hands and hurried towards the castle.

"If only everything happens as it did in my dream," he whispered when he got as far as the castle door without being stopped. He had never got so close to the castle before. He touched the door with the flower. It flew open. As he walked through the dark and cobwebby castle the witch danced round him, screeching and shouting, and casting all the spells she could think of and making up lots of new ones too. But nothing worked. The flower's magic was stronger than hers.

Presently, Joringel came to a room where seven hundred wicker cages hung from hooks in the ceiling. Sitting forlornly in each cage was a sad brown bird.

Out of seven hundred, how could he tell which was Jorinda? And then Joringel saw the witch sneaking away with one of the cages hidden in the crook of her arm. He knew at once that THAT was Jorinda. He snatched the cage from the witch and opened the door. The instant the velvety red petals of the flower brushed against the bird's wing it turned back into Jorinda.

"I knew you would come," she whispered. "I knew you would find a way of rescuing me."

Now that he had found Jorinda, Joringel set about freeing all the other little brown birds from the witch's spell. Soon there were seven hundred empty cages swinging from the ceiling.

From that day onwards, the witch lost her power to cast spells and it was safe to walk anywhere in the wood, by day, or by night.

Aladdin

Once upon a time, there was a magician, who went to China to find a magic lamp he had heard about. He knew it was hidden in an underground cave, and he knew that the only way to get into the cave was through a narrow passage. He knew too, that if the clothes of anyone passing through the passage touched the walls, they would die. He didn't want to risk his own life, even for a magic lamp, so he befriended a Chinese boy called Aladdin, and sent him into the cave.

"Wear this ring," said the magician as Aladdin got ready to climb down into the passage. "It may help to protect you."

"Protect me? Protect me from what?" asked Aladdin.

"Nothing," said the magician quickly. "There is nothing at all to be afraid of. Down you go, there's a good lad, and bring me the little lamp which you will find on the ledge at the back of the cave."

The magician was nervous, and
Aladdin seemed to be in the cave
a very long time. He was just
beginning to think Aladdin's
clothes HAD touched the walls of
the passage, and that he would
never see him again, when he saw
Aladdin's face framed in the
gloom at the end of the passage.

"Have you got it? Give it
to me!" said the magician
eagerly. "Give me the lamp!"
He reached down, and would have
snatched the lamp from Aladdin,
but Aladdin put it in his sleeve
and the magician could not reach
it. Aladdin had a feeling that
perhaps the magician was not to
be trusted, so he said,

"Help me out first, then I
will give you the lamp."

"Give me the lamp first,"
said the magician.

"Help me out first," said
Aladdin. The magician wouldn't
give in, and neither would
Aladdin. Suddenly, the magician
lost his patience and his temper.

"If you will not give me the
lamp, then you can stay in the cave
for EVER!" he shouted, and he closed
the entrance to the passage with a
short, sharp spell, and went away
fuming.

Poor Aladdin! He didn't know what to do. He sat in the dark and tried to think. Then he absent-mindedly rubbed the ring which the magician had given him before he went into the cave. There was a hiss and a strange wispy figure, wearing a turban, curled up in the air in front of him like smoke from a fire. Aladdin gasped, and shielded his eyes from the sudden light.

"Who . . . who are you?" he asked.

"I am the genie of the ring. What is your command oh master?"

"Can you take me home?" asked Aladdin.

Before Aladdin had time to blink he found himself standing outside his own house, wondering if he was asleep or awake. He knew he couldn't be dreaming when he found the lamp tucked inside his sleeve. He took it to his mother.

"We can sell this and buy food," he said.

"No one will buy a dusty old lamp," said Aladdin's mother. "Let me clean it first." She had rubbed it but once, when there was a hiss, and another strange figure appeared and wavered in the air like a wisp of smoke. Aladdin's mother was very frightened, but Aladdin asked,

"Who are you?"

"I am the genie of the lamp. What is your command oh master?"

And that's how it came about that Aladdin and his mother became rich. Whatever they wanted the genie of the lamp provided, and when Aladdin fell in love with a princess he was rich enough to marry her and take her to live in a beautiful palace.

Aladdin and his princess lived happily for a long time. They shared all their secrets, except one. Aladdin never told the princess about the magic lamp.

One day, when Aladdin was out hunting, and the princess was at home in the palace, an old pedlar called from the street,

"New lamps for old! New lamps for old!"

Now, though Aladdin had never spoken about the lamp to his princess, she had seen it, and when she heard the calls of the pedlar, who was really the wicked magician in disguise, she thought, 'I will get Aladdin a new lamp'. She ran into the street and exchanged, what she thought was a useless and broken lamp, for a bright and shining new one.

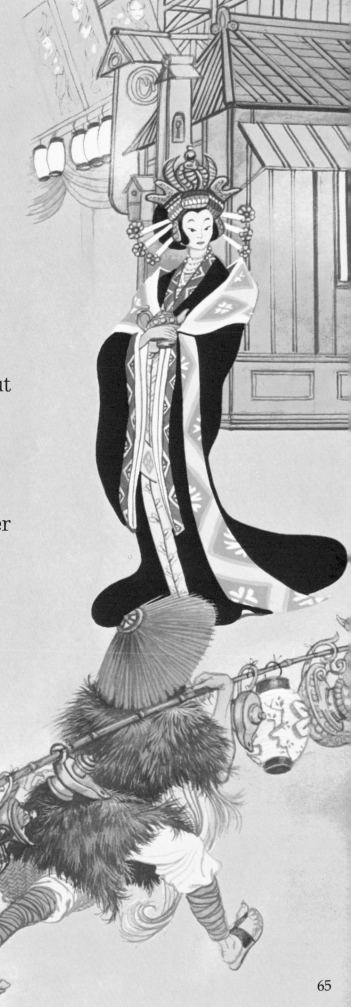

65

Immediately he had the magic lamp in his hand, the magician dropped the basket and threw off his disguise.

"He . . . he . . . he . . ." he chortled. "Now everything Aladdin has shall be mine." He summoned the genie of the lamp and ordered him to take him, Aladdin's palace and Aladdin's princess to far away Africa.

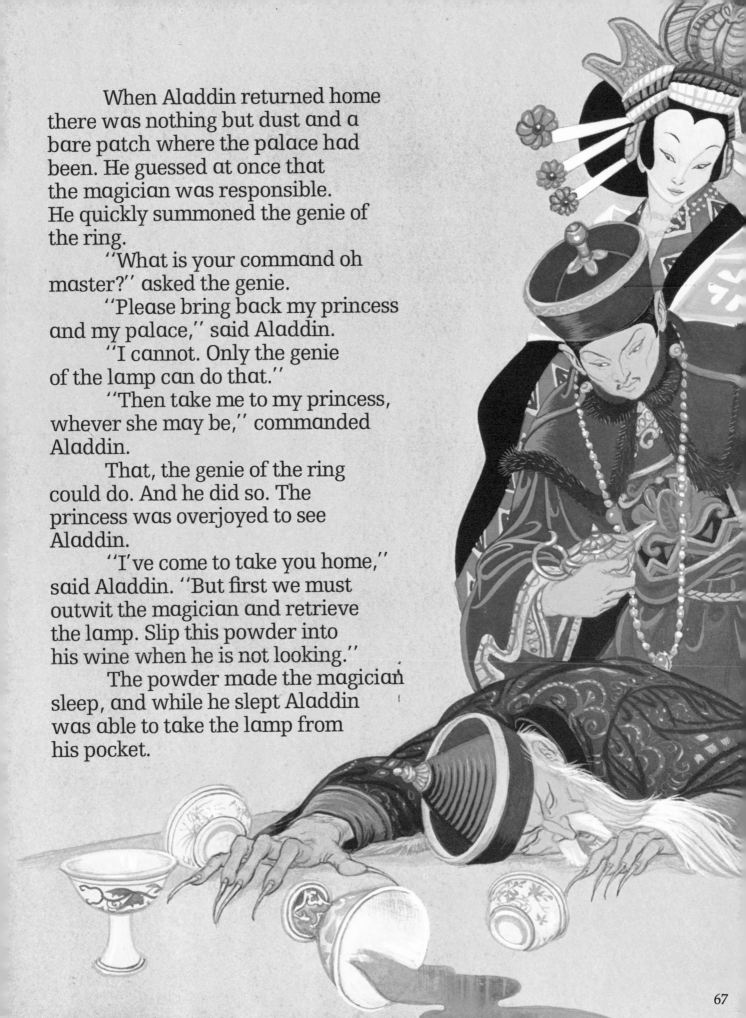

When Aladdin returned home there was nothing but dust and a bare patch where the palace had been. He guessed at once that the magician was responsible. He quickly summoned the genie of the ring.

"What is your command oh master?" asked the genie.

"Please bring back my princess and my palace," said Aladdin.

"I cannot. Only the genie of the lamp can do that."

"Then take me to my princess, whever she may be," commanded Aladdin.

That, the genie of the ring could do. And he did so. The princess was overjoyed to see Aladdin.

"I've come to take you home," said Aladdin. "But first we must outwit the magician and retrieve the lamp. Slip this powder into his wine when he is not looking."

The powder made the magician sleep, and while he slept Aladdin was able to take the lamp from his pocket.

Aladdin summoned the genie of the lamp.

"What is your command oh master?" asked the genie.

"Leave the magician here in the middle of Africa, and take the palace, and everyone else in it, back to China," said Aladdin.

And that is what the genie of the lamp did. And everyone, except the magician, who woke up and found himself on a sand dune and who is still trying to work out how he got there, lived happily ever after.

The White Dove

Once, on a cold and blustery day, a coach was travelling through the forest. It was bumping along over the ruts and through the puddles when a band of robbers ran from the trees.

"Your money or your lives!" they shouted.

As the coachman pulled hard on the reins, and the coach came to a halt, one of the doors jolted open. A slim girl, with brown hair, managed to slip unnoticed through the door and into the trees. She ran deeper and deeper into the forest, catching her dress on brambles and losing her shoes as she went. She did not stop running until the shouts of the robbers had faded away into the distance and all she could hear were the birds. And then, she sat on a fallen log, and buried her face in her hands. She was safe from the robbers it was true, but she was alone in a deep dark wood, with nowhere to go, and no one to help her.

"Oh woe is me," she sobbed. "What shall I do? I will never find my way out of the forest."

Presently, through her sobs, she heard the gentle whirr of wings. She looked up and saw a white dove hovering in front of her. It was carrying a tiny key in its beak. It dropped the key on the moss at her feet, and said,

"In the tree behind you, you will find a tiny lock. Open it with the key."

Sure enough, hidden in the bark of the tree, and so tiny that she almost missed it, was a tiny keyhole. She turned the key in it and a door opened to reveal a cupboard containing bread, and milk.

"Thank you little dove," said the girl, through her tears.

When she had eaten, the dove dropped a second key at her feet. That opened a tree door which led to a room just large enough to hold a bed.

"Sleep there, and you will be safe," said the dove.

The days passed, and whenever the girl was in need of anything the dove came to her with a key which opened yet another door in yet another tree. One day, when the dove was sitting on her hand, it said, "Will you do something for me?"

"Gladly," said the girl, stroking the dove's soft feathers.

"Then listen carefully," said the dove. "Follow the path that leads into the deepest part of the wood. It will lead you to a cottage. In the cottage you will see an old woman sitting by the fire. Do not speak to her but pass on her right side and enter the room behind her. On the table you will see many rings encrusted with jewels that sparkle like fire, and amongst them, one made of gold. Please bring me the gold ring."

The girl followed the path and found the cottage. She could see the old woman sitting by the fire.

"What are you doing?" croaked the old woman, as the girl crept past her. The girl put her hand over her mouth so that she would not be tricked into speaking. She found the table covered with jewelled rings, but of the golden ring there was no sign. And then she saw the old woman sneaking through the door with a bird-cage hidden under her shawl.

'The ring must be in the cage' thought the girl, and snatched it from the old woman. Sure enough, the bird was holding the ring in its beak. The girl took it gently, and then ran to the tree where her friend the dove had told her to wait. The dove was not there. She waited, and waited, and still the dove did not come. She leant sadly against the tree, and her tears began to fall as she thought perhaps she would never see the dove again. And then, something very strange happened. The tree felt strangely soft, for a tree . . . and then, it seemed to grow arms which wrapped themselves around her.

''Do not cry,'' said a gentle voice.

The tree was changing into a prince, and all around her other trees were changing into the prince's friends.

''Do not be afraid,'' said the Prince, for of course, the girl WAS afraid. ''The woman in the cottage is a witch. She cast a spell on us all. She turned us into trees, but because I am a prince she allowed me to fly as a dove, for two hours every day.''

He gently uncurled the girl's fingers and took the ring from her hand. ''When you took this from the witch you broke her spell.''

And then the girl recognized the voice of her dear friend the dove, and she was afraid no longer.

Like most fairy stories, this one has a happy ending too. The girl married the prince and became a princess, and they lived happily ever after.

Thumbling

There are many stories about Thumbling, the boy who was no bigger than a thumb. All adventures have to begin somewhere, and this story tells how one of Thumbling's began.

Thumbling's father was going into the forest to cut wood.

"I do wish someone could bring the cart to me when I have finished," he sighed, "then I wouldn't have to come all the way home to fetch it."

"I'll bring it to you," said Thumbling.

"How can you?" laughed Thumbling's father. "You are far too small to lead the horse."

"That may be so," said Thumbling, "but if Mother harnesses the horse for me I will sit in his ear, and tell him where to go."

It seemed a good idea, so Thumbling's father went off with his axe over his shoulder. "Make sure you're not late," he said.

"I won't be," said Thumbling.

When it was time, Thumbling's mother harnessed the horse, Thumbling climbed into the horse's ear, and off they went.

"Gee up!" cried Thumbling, who for such a small boy had an astonishingly loud voice. "Gee up!" The horse wasn't too keen on being shouted at from inside his own ear and set off at a brisk trot. "To the right!" shouted Thumbling, when he wanted the horse to go to the right. "To the left!" shouted Thumbling when he wanted him to go to the left. "Straight on!" he shouted when he wanted him to go neither to the left, nor to the right. They were almost at the place where they were to meet Thumbling's father, when they passed two men.

"That's very strange," said one of the men. "I can hear the driver of that horse and cart, but I can't see him."

"Let's follow it, and see where it goes," said his companion.

"Whoa there . . ." shouted Thumbling when they reached the clearing. "Are we in good time?"

"I've just finished," said Thumbling's father, as he lifted Thumbling from the horse's ear.

The two men nearly fell over one another in their excitement.

"If we had a little man like that we could make our fortunes," they cried. "We could show him at the fairgrounds. People would come from miles around to see him. We must buy him."

"No!" said Thumbling's father when they spoke to him. "My son is not for sale."

Now it so happened that Thumbling felt in the right mood to start a new adventure, so he climbed onto his father's shoulder and whispered,

"Let me go Father. You and Mother could use the money, and I will come back. You can be sure of that."

So, Thumbling's father, who was used to his son's ways, said the two men could take him in exchange for a bag of gold, and if they first helped him load the logs onto the cart.

"Where will you sit?" asked one of the men, when Thumbling had waved goodbye to his father.

"On the brim of your hat," said Thumbling.

"Is he still there?" asked the man who was wearing the hat, every few minutes. Because he was wearing the hat he couldn't see what was happening on the brim.

"We mustn't lose him."

Sometimes, when they checked Thumbling was at the front of the hat. Sometimes he was at the back. Sometimes he was looking where they were going. Sometimes he was looking where they had been. Sometimes he was lying on his back, looking up at the endless blue sky.

The two men walked a long way. Just as it was beginning to get dark, they sat down on a grassy bank to rest.

"Take your hat off," said Thumbling.

"Why should I do that?" asked the man wearing the hat.

"Because it's bad manners to keep your hat on ALL the time," said Thumbling. "And anyway, if you don't take your hat off sometimes your head will get too hot and your hair will fall out."

"You could be right," said the man, and took off his hat and laid it on the grass.

Quick as a grasshopper, Thumbling jumped off the brim, and ran through the grass until he came to a mousehole. Down he went.

The two men were furious.

"Come out!" they shouted. "We have been tricked!" they shouted even louder. It didn't matter how much they shouted, or how hard they poked their sticks down the mousehole, Thumbling would NOT come out. Eventually it became too dark to see where the hole was any more and they had to go home without him.

Now Thumbling was free to go where he wanted and do what he liked. He slept in the mousehole that night and next day he went to look for adventure. It was a long time before he got home again, but he did get there in the end. He always did at the end of ALL his adventures.